Bruno
and the Bees

by
Sylvie Daigneault

HarperCollinsPublishersLtd

http://www.harpercollins.com/canada

HarperCollins books may be purchased for educational, business, or sales promotional use.
For information please write: Special Markets Department, HarperCollins Canada,
55 Avenue Road, Suite 2900, Toronto, Ontario M5R 3L2.

98 99 00 First Edition 10 9 8 7 6 5 4 3 2 1

Printed and bound in Hong Kong / China
Design by DOUG PANTON INC.

Canadian Cataloguing in Publication Data

Daigneault, Sylvie
Bruno and the bees

ISBN 0-00-224552-3 (bound)
ISBN 0-00-648145-0 (pbk.)

I. Title.

PS8557.A4459B786 1998   jC813'.54   C97-932813-6
PZ7.D34B786 1998

To Alain

Lush green leaves covered the treetops like huge umbrellas. Even under the hot sun, Bruno's forest stayed moist and cool. Bruno loved summer, because there were lots of berries for him to eat.

"Hmm," he said, shoving the tasty fruit into his mouth.

"Bzzz... Bzzz... Bzzz..." Bruno's eyes opened
wide as a big furry insect landed on his nose.
"Who are you?" he asked.
"I'm Queen Bee," she said, with sparks in her
black shiny eyes.

"A queen!" said Bruno. "Do you even
live in a castle?"

"Yes, and I have a royal court, with thousands
of other bees," Queen Bee said proudly.

"Do you make honey?" he asked. Bruno
loved honey.

"Of course!" she laughed, making a quick
blur in the air as she buzzed off.

"Wait for me!" Bruno shouted, charging after her through the forest. Bruno was dreaming about the mountains of honey he would find in her castle.

Bruno followed Queen Bee so closely that, when she flew into a hole in an old chestnut tree, he bumped into the trunk.

He could hear deep humming sounds coming from inside the tree.

Looking for the honey he knew was inside the bees' nest, Bruno shoved his big nose right into the hole. Unfortunately, he didn't see the guard bees gathering for an attack until it was too late.

"Ahhh!" he screamed, as the angry bees rushed to chase him away.

Bruno reached his cave just before the bees caught him.

"What did I do wrong?" he asked his mama.

"Oh, Bruno," Clementine said softly. "The bees always share their honey with us, but you should never take it before the Queen says you may.

"You will have to apologize."

"She might like a present," said Gregory, Bruno's papa, in his big deep voice.

"But all I have are my toys," Bruno said sadly. Then he caught sight of something.

"Could I take some honey instead?"

"What a clever bear!" Gregory said affectionately, sending Bruno off with a full jar.

 Walking back through the forest, Bruno met Clara the badger.

"What do you have there?" she asked.

"Just a jar," Bruno said. "It's for..."

Before Bruno could explain, Clara had poured some honey into her cup.

"Uh oh," Bruno thought. "But maybe Queen Bee won't notice if the jar isn't *completely* full."

Saying goodbye to Clara, Bruno took the
path along the stream.

"Fish!" he thought, getting a little hungry.

"One fish dipped in the jar, two fish dipped in
honey, three fish dipped in gold!" he sang as he ate.

"Surely Queen Bee won't mind if just a *little*
bit more honey is missing."

With so many snacks in his belly, Bruno started to feel sleepy.

"I'll just have a nap," he decided, resting in the shade of an oak tree.

Pok! Pok! Two acorns bounced off Bruno's head, waking him up—just in time to see three squirrels stealing the honey jar!

"What did I get myself into?" Bruno groaned, knowing he would have to arrive at the bees' nest empty-handed. He remembered those guard bees.

Queen Bee didn't look happy to see Bruno.

"Have you come back to cause more trouble?" she asked.

Bruno tried to apologize, but Queen Bee wouldn't listen.

Bruno lay down in a patch of daisies to think about what to do next.

"The bees work so hard," he thought, watching them stuff their back legs with the sweet gold powder they used to make honey. "I wish I could help."

Then he thought harder.

"Maybe I *can* help!"

With a bow, Bruno offered a bunch of daisies to Queen Bee.

"These are for you," he said nervously. Slowly, her frown turned into a smile.

"Oh, little bear," she said. "You look just like a prince!"

"I don't mind being a prince," Bruno said. "But only if a prince is allowed to eat honey!"